In the land of Makkhipuri,

The fly was god for all,

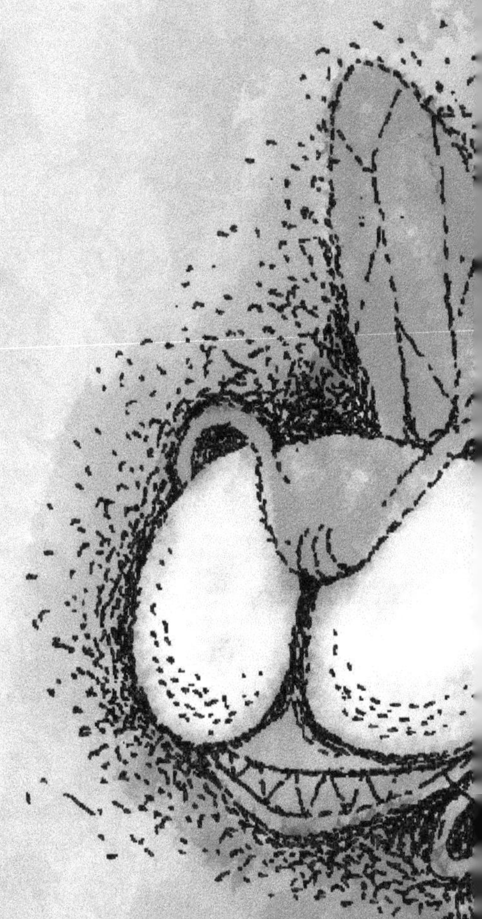

They prayed to it for good health,
They called it Makkhilal.
ALL HAIL

THE FLY!

They left their food all open,
For Makkhilal to taste,

They let the fly to sit on,
Their babies' eyes and face.

Our flying god is so kind,

The people said each day,

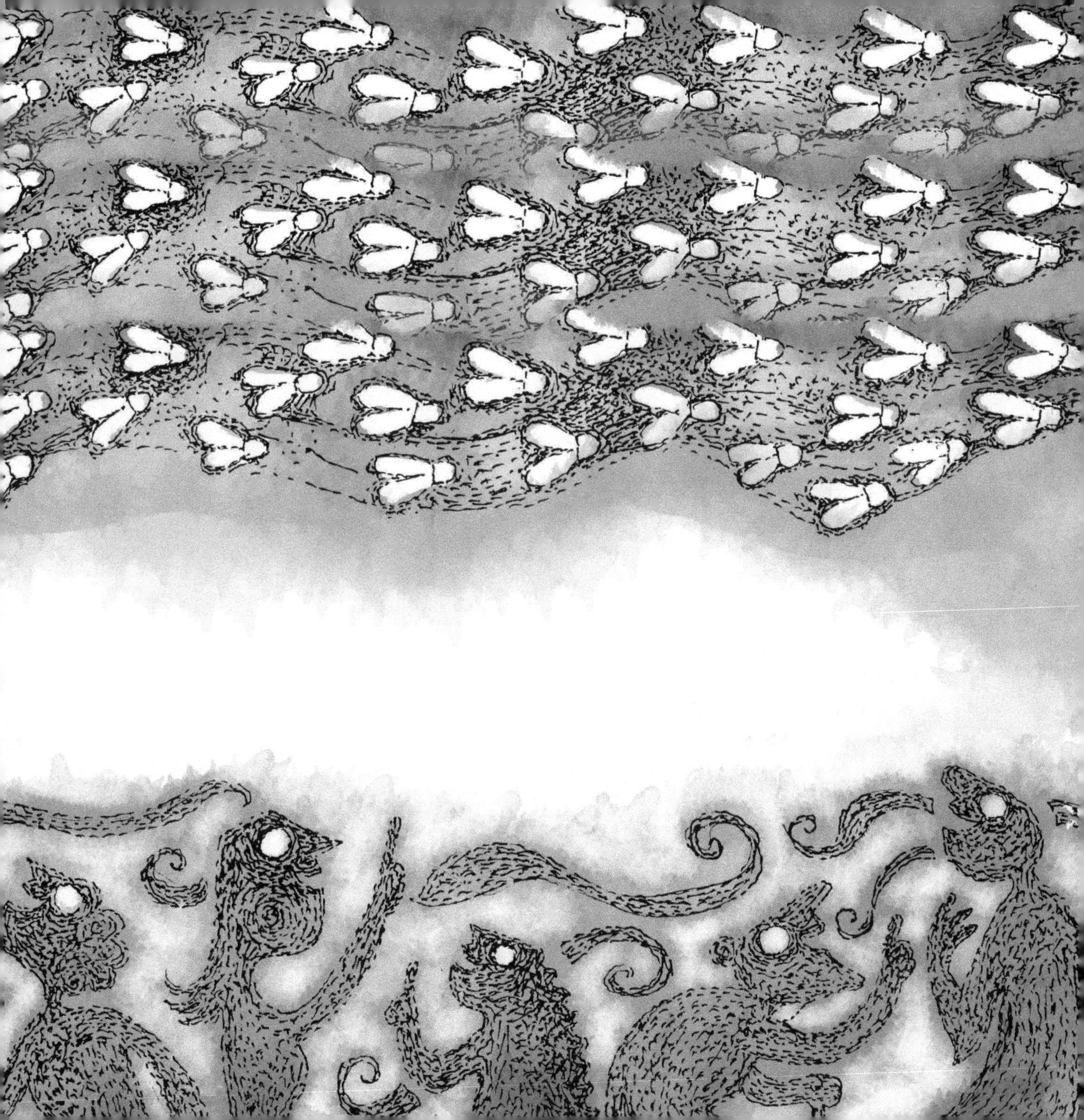

They offered prasad daily,
So Makkhilal would stay.

Why were their children dying?
What made them always sick?

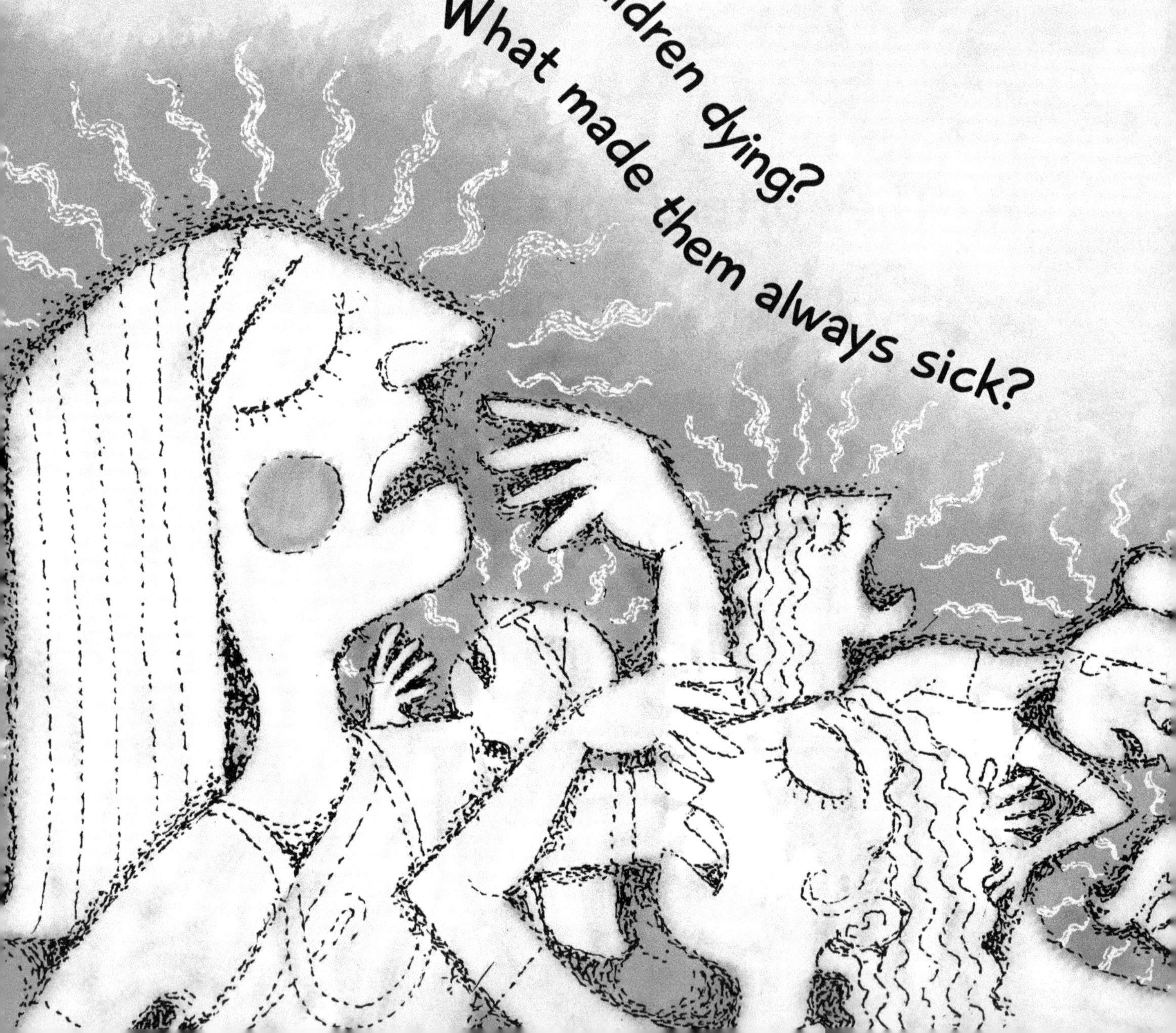

They never even wondered,
If it was Makkhi's wicked trick!

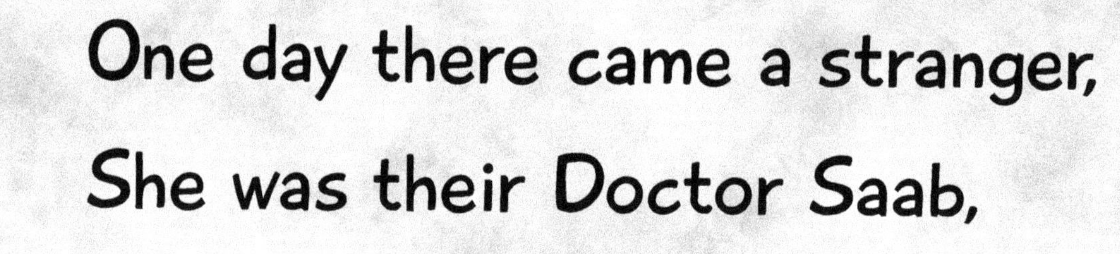

One day there came a stranger,

She was their Doctor Saab,

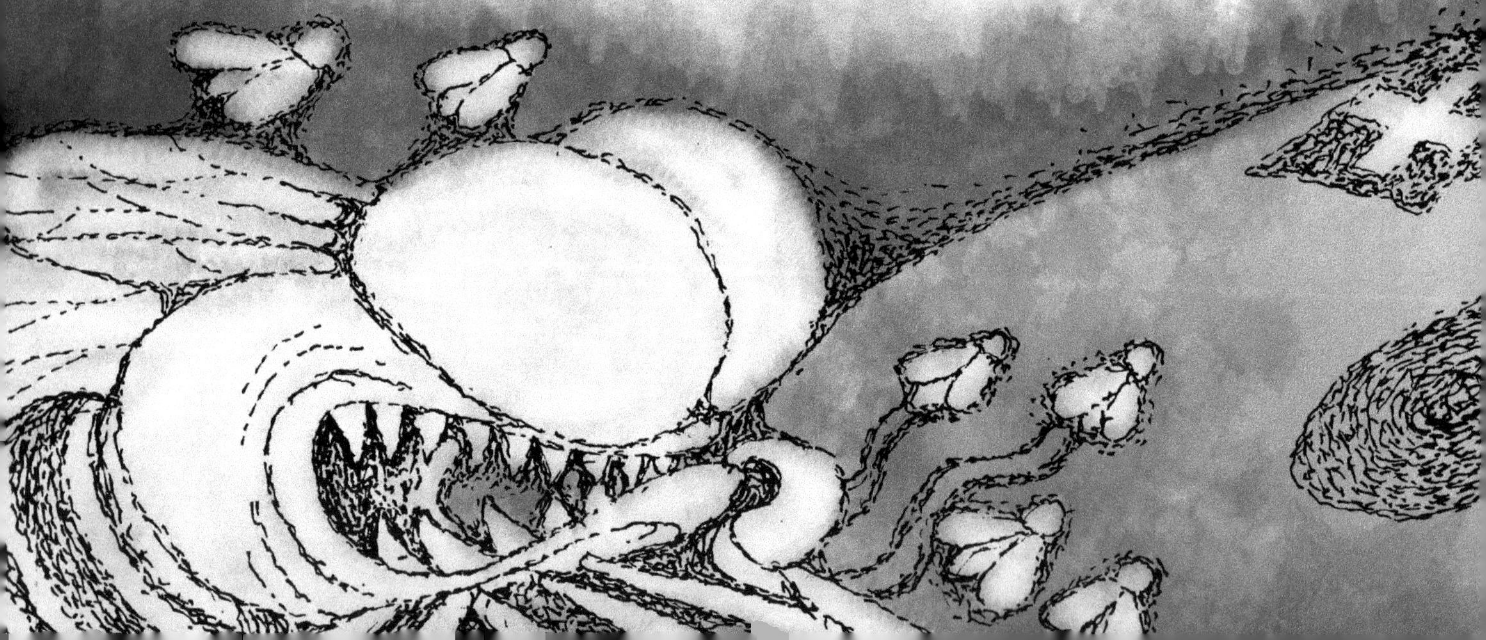

She threw the thronging flies out,

Ordered an

inquilab!

"No flies,
no flies,
no FLIES, here!"

the smart young doctor said.

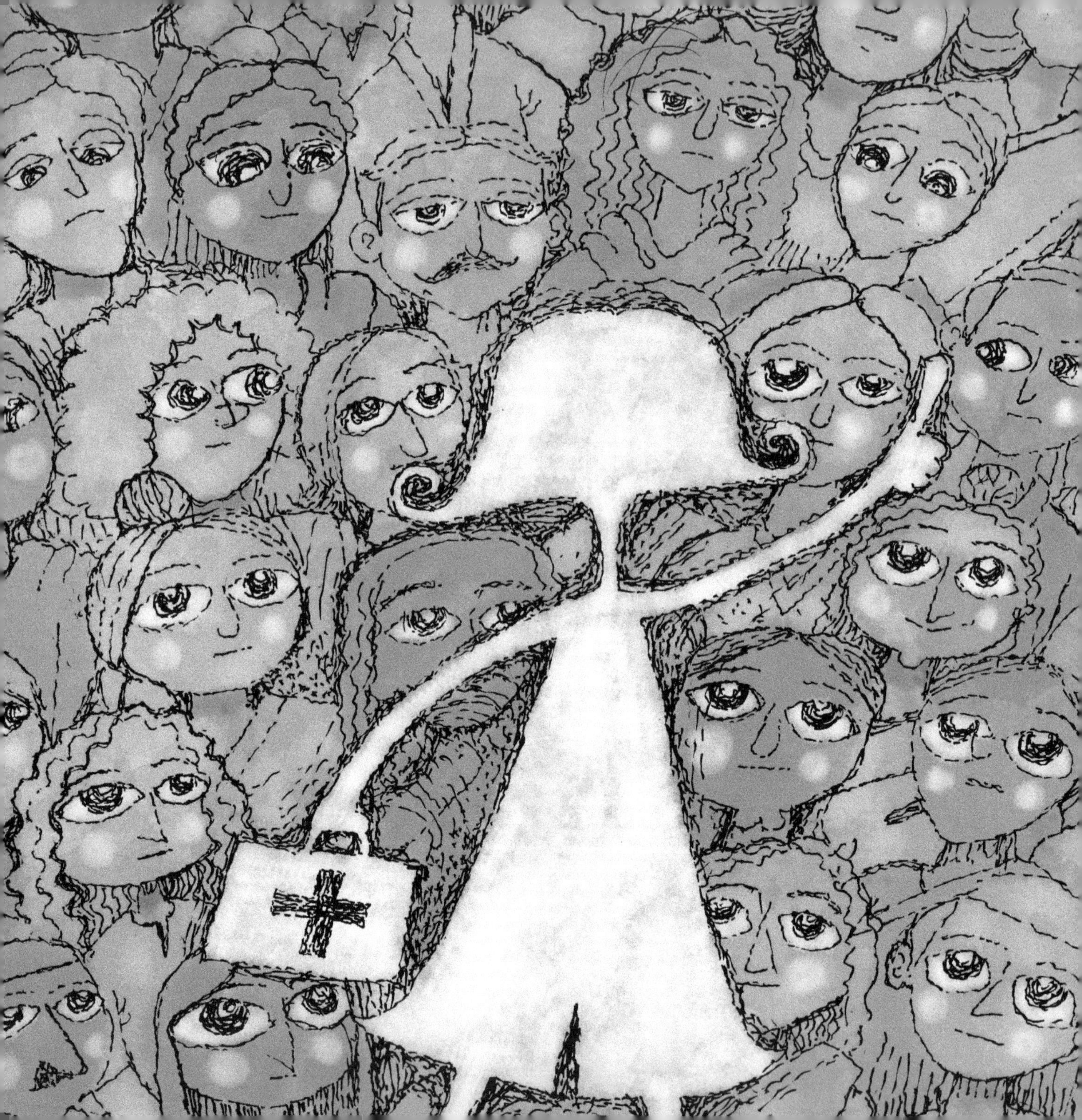

"They are the cause of diseases,
They just **MUST NOT** spread!"

No prasad for the black gods?

For Makkhilal the Fly?

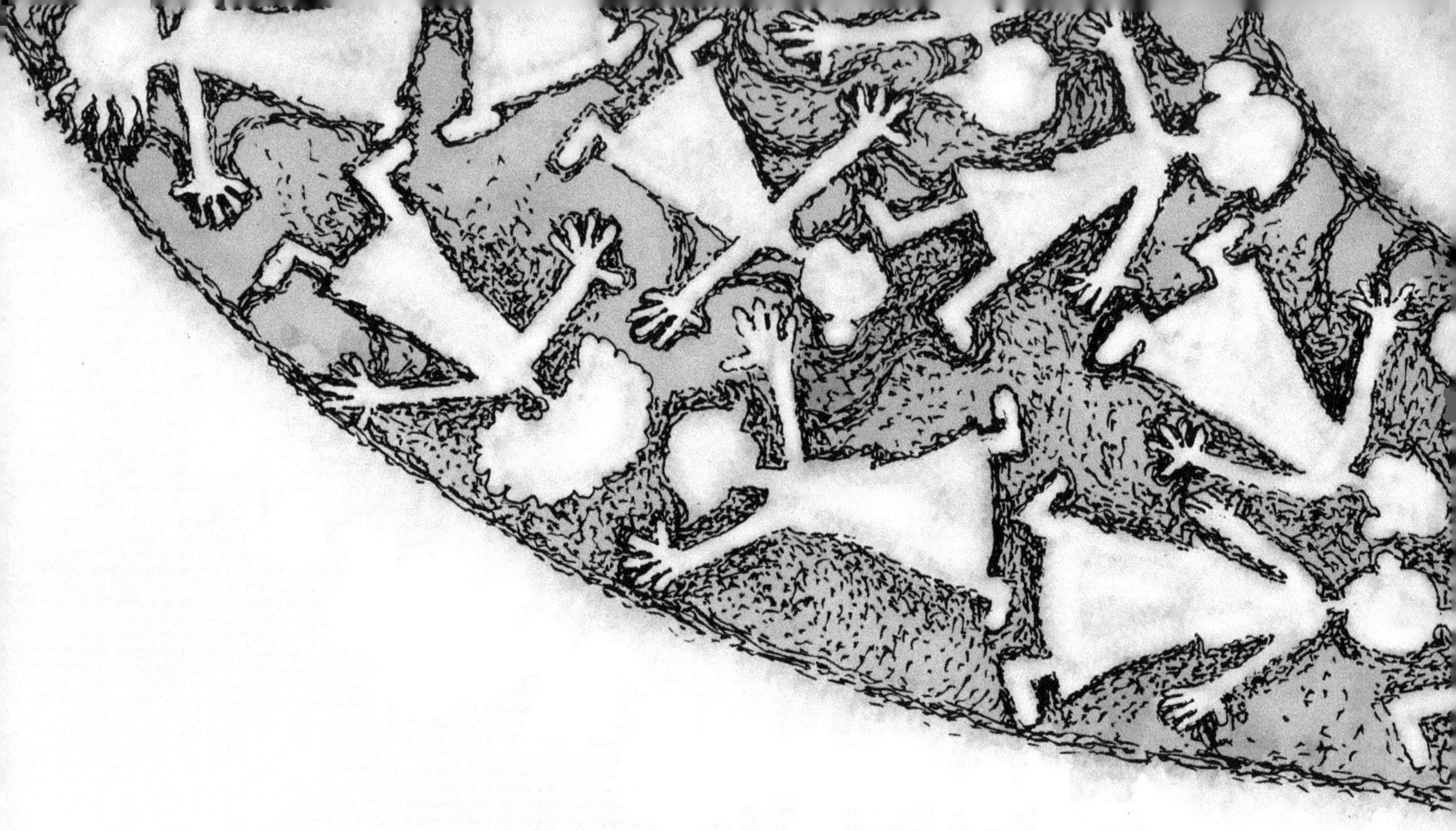

The people feared the god's curse,

They all lay down to die.

And then, guess what happened,

There was no curse, no drought ...

The children are now healthy,
They play and sing and shout!

The moral of this story,

Is not too hard to see ...

We must be careful whom we choose,
Our god or king to be!

1 There are over **100,000** species of flies in the world! That's a huge lot, don't you think?

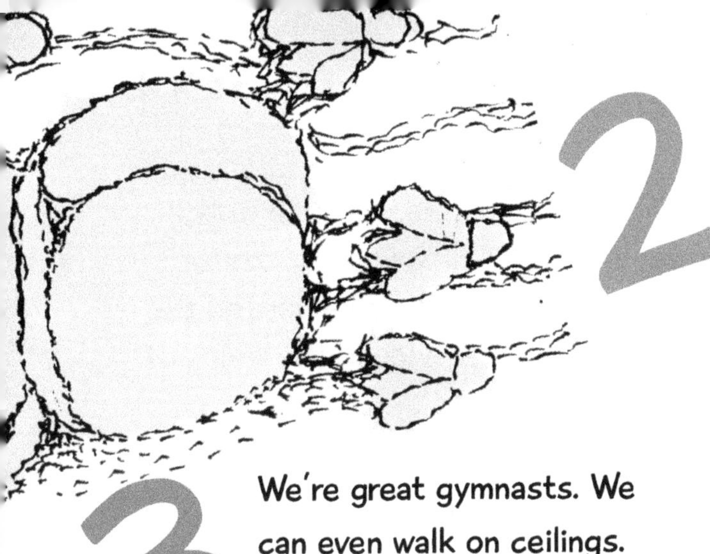

2 We, the houseflies, are the most common species of flies.

3 We're great gymnasts. We can even walk on ceilings. Pretty cool, isn't it?

4 People don't call us "houseflies" because we're their pet flies but because we like to get inside their houses!

5 But we have disgusting taste in food—garbage juice, rotten fruits, vegetable scraps, anyone?

6 Because we walk on garbage, germs get stuck to our feet and we can cause hundreds of diseases — from diarrhoea to flu!

7 So, the next time you don't want to share your food with us, keep it covered.

8 Don't forget to wash your hands before having your food. And never eat food that has fallen onto the floor.

A SUPER DRINK

Diarrhoea can be dangerous — it can cause dehydration, or extreme loss of water from your body. Here's an easy way to prepare a super drink that can treat dehydration.

How to make ORS (Oral Rehydration Solution):

1. Mix 6 teaspoons of sugar in 5 cups of water. **2.** Add half a teaspoon of salt to it. **3.** Your ORS is ready! **4.** Have this super drink 6-8 times a day to keep your body hydrated.

Geeta Dharmarajan loves writing stories for children. She was one of the editors of *Target,* a magazine for children, and *The Pennsylvania Gazette*, the magazine of the University of Pennsylvania. She has been awarded the prestigious Padma Shri in 2012 for her distinguished service in the fields of literature and education.

Charbak Dipta is an Oxford alumnus and an award-winning illustrator, a foodie and a globetrotter.

KATHA

First published in Tamasha! by Katha, 1994

ISBN 978-93-88284-79-0

Our Mission: Every child reading well for fun and meaning!

KATHA is a registered nonprofit organization started in 1988. We work in the literacy to literature continuum. Devoted to enhancing the joys of reading amongst children and adults, we work with more than 1,00,000 children in poverty, to bring them to grade-level reading through quality books and interventions.

A3, Sarvodaya Enclave, Sri Aurobindo Marg, New Delhi 110 017

Phone: 4141 6600 . 4182 9998 . 2652 1752

E-mail: marketing@katha.org, Website: www.katha.org, www.books.katha.org

Ten per cent of sales proceeds from this book will support the quality education of children studying in Katha schools.
Katha regularly plants trees to replace the wood used in the making of its books.

www.ingramcontent.com/pod-product-compliance
Ingram Content Group UK Ltd.
Pitfield, Milton Keynes, MK11 3LW, UK
UKHW061826190726
13853UKWH00009B/2449

9 789388 284790